In this glossary:

[a] is pronounced as in far
[e] is pronounced as in get
[ee] is pronounced as in feet
[i] is pronounced as in sit
[o] is pronounced as between got and goat
[oo] is pronounced as in loose
[y] is pronounced as in yes

[kh] is pronounced as in Scottish loch
[zh] is pronounced as in vision

Other books available from Ethnic Enterprises

Ukrainian Folk Tales Retold in English:

6. Oil in the Borsch
5. The Worry Imps
4. Boris Threeson
3. How April Went to Visit March
2. Zhabka
1. The Raspberry Hut

Humorous stories of the old days:

Vuiko Yurko Second-Hand Stories
Vuiko Yurko The First Generation

Baba the Cook

I Can't Find the Words to Tell You

Kharkiv

Dream Star Stories

From the Gallows
The Lost Testimony of Louis Riel

Carrots to Coins

and Other Ukrainian Folk Tales
Retold in English

Retold by Danny Evanishen
Translations by J Zurowsky
Illustrations by Ralph Critchlow

Published by
Ethnic Enterprises
Publishing Division
Summerland, BC

Canadian Cataloguing in Publication Data

Evanishen, Danny, 1945-
 Carrots to coins, and other Ukrainian folk tales retold in
English

ISBN 0-9681596-3-X

1. Tales--Ukraine. I. Zurowsky, J., 1954- II. Title.
GR203.8.E932 2000 398.2'09477 C00-910277-9

Ethnic Enterprises
Publishing Division
Box 234
Summerland, BC
V0H 1Z0
http://www.ethnic.bc.ca

Printed and Bound in Canada
by New Horizon Printers, Summerland, BC

1 2 3 4 5 6 7 8 9 10• 09 08 07 06 05 04 03 02 01 2000

Table of Contents

Dedicated to the memory of my father,
John W Evanishen.

Foreword

This book is the seventh volume in this series. There will be more books as long as I have the stories to fill them. That should not be a problem; the Ukrainian culture is very rich in this way, and there are thousands of tales.

I enjoy collecting and publishing these stories, but they are sometimes hard to find. Many people know the stories, but for various reasons, don't get around to writing them down or recording them.

In this day and age, writing down the stories is becoming more and more important, as the people who know the stories either die or forget the stories. It is up to us, now, to save this very important part of our heritage.

As in the first six volumes of the series, some of the tales to be found in this book are old favorites, while others are less familiar.

If anyone has tales they would like to contribute to future volumes, please send them to me at this address:

Danny Evanishen
Box 234
Summerland, BC
V0H 1Z0.
devanishen@img.net
—Danny Evanishen, Publisher

Acknowledgments

In this book, some of the translations from Ukrainian were done by my father John W Evanishen and by J Zurowsky. Natalka Evanishen, my mother, provided my very first folk tales and always had lots of encouragement for me. Ralph Critchlow did the art work.

The photograph on the back cover was taken by Melva Armstrong of the WHOLife Journal at http://www.wholife.com.

Thanks are always due to the libraries and archives across Canada that make their material available. A list of all the stories and their sources will eventually be published.

When the stories submitted by various people across the country are published, I will acknowledge their contributions.

In this volume we have versions of stories submitted to me by the following people: Michael Shklanka (*Carrots to Coins, The Daughter of the Blacksmith, The Miracle of the Fire*), Norman Harris (*The Death of Kniaz Oleh*) and Nicholas J Sabulka (*The Death of Kniaz Oleh, The Gold Fish, The Phantom Turkey*).

Thank you to everyone who sent their stories in to me, thinking I would find them interesting. I definitely find them interesting.

— Danny Evanishen, Publisher

Carrots to Coins

Once, Jesus and His disciples happened to arrive at a town where a wedding was in progress. The disciples wanted to join in the celebrations, but the custom was that guests would donate money to pay the musicians as they were welcomed at the door. The disciples therefore would require money to pay the musicians as they were greeted.

They asked Jesus what to do for money. He told them to cut some carrots into coin-size slices, which they did. Jesus blessed the slices and transformed them into money and gave some to each of them.

While everyone was feasting and enjoying the entertainment, Peter, one of the disciples, became greedy. He thought he would like some coins for himself. He sneaked away to the garden, sliced some carrots, blessed them in

11

exactly the same way as Jesus had done and, lo and behold, they changed into coins.

He returned to the celebration just as everyone was donating money to the musicians by dropping their coins into a large drum. When Peter dropped his donation into the drum, instead of the jingling of coins, there was a booming sound. The musicians noticed this immediately but did nothing except watch him until nightfall, when they decided to beat him to teach him a lesson about donating carrots instead of money.

Jesus and Peter slept in a small shed with no door. Jesus was near the wall and Peter lay next to Him. Just as they fell asleep, the musicians sneaked in and beat Peter with sticks and ran out. Peter asked if he could change places with Jesus, because he thought that the musicians might return to give him another beating. Jesus agreed.

In the meantime, the musicians decided that they might as well give a beating to the other man sleeping next to the wall, just in case they had made a mistake and beat the wrong man the first time.

They went in and gave a good beating to the man by the wall. So Peter got it again.

This was a lesson to Peter not to try to do what only Jesus Himself could do, and not to try to outsmart Jesus.

A Clever Trick

A poor man named Semion went to the landlord to borrow some rye for seeding.

"I cannot lend it to you," said the lord, "because you would not pay me back."

"What? Would I not return it?" asked the poor man.

"You are poor and you have nothing to repay me with."

The poor man thought a bit and said:

"Are not the poor to live on this earth? Who knows — maybe the poor man will some day be treated with more respect and honor than the rich man."

"How can it be?" responded the lord. "No matter which house I enter, they immediately place me at the head of the table and lend me whatever I need."

"Ah, but before they sit you down, they will have sat me down first," said the poor man.

The lord was getting so angry that he could not stand in one spot. "How can it be that such a ragged man would be more respected than I? Let us make a bet! If they treat you better than they treat me, anywhere, I will give you a pair of oxen. If they treat me better, then you and your wife must work for me for one year for nothing."

"Good," said the poor man. "But where shall we go?"

"Let us go to the priest," said the lord. He knew the priest treated him with great respect.

They went to the home of the priest, where the rich man bowed low and asked that the priest lend him a wagon of oats.

"Good," said the priest. "I shall get dressed and fill the wagon."

"Thank you, good Father."

Then the priest asked the poor man, "And you, Semion. What do you need?"

The poor man came closer, put his lips to the ear of the priest and whispered, "Yesterday I dug up a barrel of gold in the forest. I want to ask you, Father, to bless it."

The priest immediately became much happier and quickly said to the lord, "You go and wait outside because I have to talk with Semion right now."

The surprised lord went outside while the priest spoke to Semion, "Well, and how do you expect me to bless that barrel?"

"I want you to come to my place and do it there. That is easier."

"No, it will be easier here. You know that when I am travelling with all my outfit, the neighbors will see and they will want to know what is going on. It is better here, Semion."

"Well then, let it be. You know more about these things than I do. I will go get the gold."

"No, wait. A good deed needs to be treated with good mead. Sit closer to the table."

Semion sat at the head of the table with the priest beside him. The wife of the priest brought in a bowl of fried fish and placed on the table a jug of whisky. Semion looked at all this and stroked his moustache happily.

Goblet after goblet the priest poured for himself and Semion. The wife also brought a drink to her lips a number of times. But though Semion drank, he did not drink away his mind. When the priest raised his goblet, Semion raised his, clinked goblets loudly with the priest and said, loudly enough for the lord to hear, "Good health to you, Father!"

The lord stood outside the door listening, and he reddened with anger. He finally saw that he had lost the bet, and stormed home.

After the snack, Semion got up, thanked the priest and said, "Now I will bring the gold."

"Good," said the priest, "but do hurry!"

With dignity the poor man stepped across the threshold and went along the road, not after the gold, but after the oxen of the lord.

He took the oxen as payment, snapped the whip and said, "Hey, you mighty oxen, your big-bellied lord will not see you any more! Hey, mighty grey ox, mighty dark ox, may the lord and the priest now realize how clever a trickster is poor Semion!"

And the priest waited and waited for Semion and his barrel of gold, and he is waiting to this day.

The Daughter of the Blacksmith

In a village along their route, Jesus and His disciples stopped at a blacksmith shop. The daughter of the blacksmith came in to see who was there.

Jesus saw that her face was badly disfigured. The blacksmith told Him that she was born that way. Because of this she had not had any suitors and would likely spend the rest of her life as an old maid, even though she was a kind and industrious girl.

Jesus took pity on the girl and told her father that she would have a beautiful face if she bent over the glowing charcoal and received a slight blast from the bellows.

She agreed and bent her face over the coals. Jesus gave the bellows a slight blast.

When she raised her head, her face was miraculously transformed. She was a radiant, most beautiful maiden.

This procedure and transformation happened to be seen by a man passing by. This man had an ordinary-looking wife, but always wished that she were more beautiful to show off to people.

When he got home, he told his wife what he had seen, and convinced her to come to the blacksmith shop and become beautiful.

When they arrived at the blacksmith shop, the blacksmith was there alone, and he let them do as they pleased. The wife leaned over the coals and the husband gave the bellows one big powerful blast. After the smoke cleared, the wife was hardly recognizable. Her face was scarred and unsightly.

This taught them a lesson to accept and be thankful for what they had.

Death as a Godmother

In a certain village lived a poor man named Yatsko. All his worldly wealth amounted to a hut by the forest, and he supported his wife and himself through the work of his hands. A daughter was born to them and they wanted to baptize her in church.

Yatsko went to his rich neighbors to ask them to be godparents, but the rich man declined, saying that he was not well.

A second neighbor excused himself, saying that he had no time because he had to go to the forest for firewood.

The third answered that he had to plow and sow his fields because it was already time, and the weather would not wait.

The rejection by all the rich neighbors so hurt poor Yatsko that, as he walked toward home, he complained loudly:

"They snub me because I am poor, or maybe they fear that I will ask them for help. Oh, how unfortunate I am that I must baptize my child without godparents! If I were rich, I would be honored to be a godparent for all, and I would happily bring all of them to the Cross."

Saddened because of his fate, he began to cry. Then he saw a woman approaching him, and he greeted her,

"Praise Jesus Christ!"

She replied,

"Praise Him forever! Why are you so worried, Yatsko?"

He explained to her how no one would be godparents because he was poor.

"You have nothing to worry about, Yatsko, because the rich ones declined. God is the richest of all and loves all people the same whether they be rich or poor, as long as they live an honorable life. You are a good man; therefore God will not abandon you but will reward you with what you need for your happiness. If you want me to be the godmother and the gravedigger the godfather, then come to the church tomorrow. I will be there and we will ask the priest to baptize your daughter. Now go home and tell your wife!"

Saying this, she disappeared.

Yatsko went home and told his wife what had happened. The more he thought, the more confidence he gained and, finally, he stopped worrying altogether.

Early next day the newborn girl was taken to church. There the family met the woman, who was dressed better than the richest villager. She and the gravedigger held the child for the baptism, blessing her so she would grow in happiness, health and joy. When they left the church, the woman told Yatsko:

"As a gift for the child I will not give you money but, Kum, you shall receive from me another gift which will make you wealthy. From this time on, you will be a famous healer. Money will flow into your pocket like water.

"Take this little box of powder. When you are called to a sickroom and see me there, pretend not to notice. If I stand by the feet of the sick person, take a pinch of the powder, mix it in a spoon of well-water and give it to the patient to drink. He will immediately get better. News of such a miracle cure will spread throughout the whole world. Thus, people will recognize you and praise you.

"But remember, Kum, do not try to save the patient if I stand by his head. Then you must say that there is no hope for him; may he prepare to be joined with God and his ancestors. May he prepare for Death. Remember well what I have told you, Yatsko, for I myself am Death! Farewell!"

At that moment Death disappeared and Yatsko returned home. The beautiful child behaved wonderfully and Yatsko became noted as a miracle-working doctor. He did not work in the fields any more but travelled from village to village, healing the sick and making money.

One day, Yatsko was called to a castle where a prince was ill. The most famous doctors had been brought in, but none was able to cure the prince, who was dying. When the doctors gave up and said that the prince must die, then Yatsko was summoned.

When Yatsko entered the room of the sick prince, the princess kneeled at his feet and begged him to save the prince. In return, she would cover him with gold.

Yatsko saw Death by the head of the sick man, warning him not to try to save the patient. But the promise of gold awoke greed within Yatsko, and he thought long about what to do. Finally, he told the attendants to turn the bed around so that the feet of the prince were where his head had been, and his head was where the feet had been.

Death then found herself standing by the feet of the prince and, shaking her fist at Yatsko, she disappeared.

Yatsko quickly mixed up a pinch of his powder in a spoon of well-water and gave it to the prince, who immediately became better.

An immeasurable joy reigned throughout the castle. The prince hugged and kissed Yatsko, calling him his friend. He lodged him in the castle and brought in his wife and children. He gave them a large apartment and they ate at the same table.

However, not all the rich fare tasted good to Yatsko, because lords are forever eating food which the peasant never touches, like frogs, snails and other such things.

Seeing this, the prince asked Yatsko if he would like to have an estate where he could live as he pleased.

Yatsko replied that this is what he wished for: to have nice buildings and large fields, because that would make him happy.

The prince gave him what he desired. Yatsko became involved in working the land, since he had lost the power to heal people when he saved the prince. When Death disappeared, it was forever, and Yatsko never saw her again.

But Yatsko had saved much money and had a nice farm, and thus the family lived happily. The children were well raised.

When the time came, the goddaughter of Death married a lord. At that wedding, besides the prince, there were many lords, princes and peasants to celebrate her happiness.

❖

The Death of Kniaz Oleh

In ages past, Kniaz Oleh was the ruler of Kyivan Rus, which eventually became Ukraine. So great was his fame in all the lands that tribes everywhere bowed to his will.

As Oleh aged, he became interested in life and death, especially his own. Wondering when and how he would meet his fate, he called to him the ablest of the sorcerers and vorozhkas in the land.

The oldest vorozhka soon had the answer. She told Oleh, "Great art thou, Kniaz warrior. Under siege by your enemies, Death will not greet you, nor will disease or old age cut your days short. The cause will, instead, be your beloved horse."

Hearing this, Oleh decided to retire the horse from active service, thinking that if he did not come near the horse, it could not kill him.

To this end, he gave the horse to a trusted servant, with orders that the horse was to be fed the best of grain and cared for as befits a beloved old friend.

Oleh then took a new horse and rode off to many more battles. Returning from a lengthy campaign, he remembered his old horse and went to the stable to inquire as to its health.

"Your horse passed away peacefully some time ago, Sire. His bare bones have for a long while been washed by the rains and dried by the winds on the grave mound on the steppe," said the servant.

Oleh went to the grave mound to pay his last respects to his faithful old horse. He put one foot on the bleached skull of the horse and said, "My vorozhka lied. Here is all that is left of my beloved horse. I have come back and found only its skull, and I am yet very much alive."

As Oleh said this, a poisonous snake slithered out of the skull, wrapped itself tightly around his leg and bit him. And thus, say the Chroniclers of old, Oleh died and the prophecy was indeed fulfilled.

The Fly that Plowed a Field

One morning a man hitched up his two oxen and went to plow his field. He did not notice, of course, a fly that had attached itself to one of the oxen. The fly sat on the ox and rode on it all the way to the field. While the team was plowing, the fly gave nobody any peace. It spent the whole time buzzing around first one ox and then the other.

In the evening the man turned the team homeward and the fly settled on the horn of one ox and rode home in style. On the road they met another fly who was going by. The new fly landed next to the first.

"Well, neighbor, where have you been all day?" asked the new fly.

"I am so tired," puffed the first fly. "We have been plowing the field all day long."

The other fly burst out laughing.

"I have no doubt that some of you were, but not all of you," he said. "I would watch my bragging if I were you. I see that you are good at wagging your tongue, but I have yet to see you plow a field!"

The Fox and the Bear

Little Sister Fox saw Brother Bear in his garden one day. She said to the Bear, "Please, Brother Bear, may I use some of your garden so I can plant some vegetables for myself?"

"Very well. If you share the vegetables with me, I will let you use my garden," said Brother Bear.

"Excellent," replied the Fox. "I will give you the nice green tops of the vegetables and I will keep the dirty roots."

The Bear agreed, and the Fox planted some turnips. The turnips grew very well and, when they were ready, the Fox said, "Come, Bear. It is time to share my crop. You take your green tops and I will dig up my roots."

The Bear took the tops home but soon found that they were of no use to him. The tops could not be eaten, and they were no good for anything else. He returned to the garden to see if there were any roots left, but the plot was bare. Realizing that he had been tricked, the Bear grew angry.

When the next spring came around, the Fox again asked the Bear to use some of his garden. "Oh no," said the Bear. "You used my garden last year and you tricked me. I got nothing for the use of my garden."

"If you were unhappy with the way we shared my crop last year, we can divide it the other way around this year," said the clever Fox. "This year you may have the roots and I will take the tops."

This sounded like a good plan to the Bear, and he accepted. The clever Fox planted poppies this year instead of turnips. She tended the plants, she watered them, she weeded them and, when they were ripe, she called the Bear, "Come, Bear, let us share my crop."

The Fox gathered up all the poppies and hurried home with them. The Bear was once more left with nothing. "You have tricked me again," roared the Bear. He was very angry.

The next spring, the Fox once more asked the Bear to use some of his garden. Brother Bear said, "Oh no, Little Sister Fox. The last two years you tricked me and repaid my kindness with nothing. This year you can go someplace else."

"Oh please, Brother Bear, let us forget our faults of last year. I will let you choose how we are to share my crop this year."

"Oh, very well, but I should know better," said the Bear. "This year I will take both the topmost part and the bottommost of your crop."

The Fox planted corn. She tended the plants and cared for the corn and, when it was ready, she called the Bear, "Come, Brother Bear. Let us share my crop."

The Fox gave the Bear the tops of the corn and the roots, keeping for herself the ears, which were in the middle. The Bear was so angry that he stomped off home without saying a word, and he never let the Fox share his garden again.

The Foxes in the Vineyard

Once there was a man who owned a small vineyard. When spring arrived, he went to the vineyard to see what needed to be done. He looked around and made note of everything.

"Tomorrow I will come with a hoe and take care of the weeds," he said.

A family of young foxes heard what the man said and they became very frightened. When Mother Fox came home, they hurried to tell her the news.

"There was a man here, Mother, who said he would come tomorrow and hoe the weeds. We will have to run away from our home."

"You have nothing to worry about, my children," said Mother Fox. "That man is the owner of the vineyard. I know him well, and he will not come soon."

One day much later the man returned to the vineyard. He had a hoe over his shoulder, but he quickly realized that it would not be of much use to him. He was surprised to see that the grass had grown so tall that the hoe would not do the job.

"I cannot do anything with a hoe," he said. "I will go home and get a scythe."

The young foxes were alarmed. "Mother," they cried. "The man was here again. He said he was going to go home and get a scythe. He will come back and kill us all."

"Do not be afraid," said Mother Fox. "Just play your games and do not even think about him. He will not be back soon."

Months later the man returned to the vineyard with a scythe. However, by this time the grass had grown so tall and the weeds were so tangled that by now his work was really cut out for him.

"This is too much work," he said. "I will go home and get some matches. It will be much easier to burn this trash than cut it."

"Now, my children, we must flee," said Mother Fox. "Burning the weeds takes no effort, and the man is sure to do that."

The Girl Who Wept Pearls

In the woods stood a cottage and, in the cottage, lived a man and his wife. They desperately wanted a child, so they began to pray to God to give them one. They beseeched God, and He gave them a daughter. She grew and prospered under their care.

The son of the tsar of their country was out hunting in the woods one day and he chanced upon the cottage in the woods. He ordered his attendant to go there to get him some water to drink.

As it happened, the attendant entered the cottage just at a time when the child was weeping, and he was astounded to see that when she wept, pearls rolled from her eyes. When the mother pacified the child she smiled, and flowers of many kinds bloomed all around the cottage.

The servant returned to the tsarevich and told him what he had just seen. The tsarevich went into the cottage to see for himself. He teased the child and she cried pearls. When she was soothed by her mother and again became happy, the flowers bloomed.

The tsarevich was quite amazed by all this and thereafter made it a point to ride by the cottage so that he could visit with the girl and her parents. As the girl grew she learned to embroider and was soon making handkerchiefs with beautiful eagles on them.

Finally, when she was of age, the tsarevich informed her father that he wished to marry the girl. Permission was gladly granted, for the father knew the tsarevich loved the girl.

The tsar, however, was angry when he heard of what his son intended. "Where are your wits, that you wish to marry a peasant girl?" he cried.

The tsarevich showed his father one of the handkerchiefs the girl had embroidered, and the impressed tsar changed his mind immediately. "Marry her, my son," he said. "Marry her."

The tsarevich went with his entourage to fetch the girl. In his company there was a jealous and very wicked old woman who also had a daughter. She had always hoped that her daughter would marry the tsarevich.

At one stopping place on the journey to the palace, the old woman seized the intended bride, blinded her and thrust her into a cave. She then put her own daughter in the place of the young girl. The tsarevich recognized only the clothing the girl was wearing and married the daughter of the wicked old woman.

Shortly after, an old man was gathering firewood in the forest. He stopped and stared when he saw a young girl in front of a cave with a large pile of pearls at her feet. He drew near and she told him her story. He felt sorry for her and took her to his home, along with the pearls, of course.

At the home of the old man, the girl told him to take the pearls to town to sell. "There is in the town a woman who has great need of pearls to carry on a deception," she said, and she described the wicked old woman. "If she approaches you to buy the pearls, do not sell them to her but say to her, 'You may have them but you must give what you have about you.'"

In town the old man met the old woman. "Sell me your pearls," she said as soon as she saw them. "How much do you want for them?"

"You may have them but you must give what you have about you," was his reply.

She gave him one of her eyes and took the pearls. The old man went home and gave the eye to the girl. She took the eye, put it in place of one of her own and began to embroider a beautiful handkerchief.

She then sent the old man back to the town with more pearls. Again he was approached by the old woman, who said, "Sell me the pearls. You must sell me the pearls."

"Very well. Give me what you have about you and you may have them."

The old woman gave him her other eye and took the pearls. The old man took the eye back to the girl, who now had both eyes. She finished embroidering her handkerchief, which was the most beautiful anyone had ever seen.

The girl then sent the old man to the palace, where a big feast was about to be held. She told him to take a bowl and beg for some soup. She then tied her beautiful handkerchief around his neck, and he left.

At the castle, the old man approached the tsarevich with his bowl, and the tsarevich immediately recognized the handiwork in the handkerchief. "Who are you? Where did you get this?" he demanded.

The old man answered, "I live in a cottage near the village, and the handkerchief was made by a young lady who is staying with me. We would like to beg some soup from you."

"Tell me of the young lady who made this beautiful handkerchief," commanded the tsarevich eagerly.

"She is a girl who was blind when I found her by the cave in the woods."

The tsarevich took the handkerchief and cried, "It is she! It is she!" He threw the old woman and her daughter out of the castle and sent them to tend the pigs. Then he went to the cottage with the old man where he found his beloved. They returned to the castle, where they were married.

The Gold Fish

Nykola liked to fish in the River Prut early in the morning. Of course, there were times when he caught no fish, but he enjoyed every moment he spent there in serenity and peace. Fishing was not only a form of relaxation for him, but it also provided a welcome change in the diet of his family.

One morning Nykola went to his favorite fishing spot, sat on a rock and threw his hook into the stream. Almost immediately a fish struck. It was a big fish, and Nykola had much trouble getting it to shore. This fish was certainly the biggest caught by anyone in his village. As he dragged the fish onto the shore, it spoke to Nykola.

"Please sir," said the fish, "I beg you to release me. I am the oldest of a large school of fish in this area, and my absence will greatly affect their well-being. If you release me, I will reward you handsomely."

Nykola was stunned. Who ever heard of a talking fish, except in fairy tales?

"Please do not tell me that you are going to grant me three wishes, for I would not believe that. I am impressed with your ability to speak, however," said Nykola.

The fish replied, "I plead with you; I have been out of the water for too long now. Please release me. I promise that I will reward you well if you do so. Come to this same spot early tomorrow morning and I will bring you something of great value."

Nykola was reluctant to set free the largest fish he had ever caught, but his sympathy for the poor fish overcame his pride. He put the fish back into the water ever so gently, and watched the fish slip away into the depths of the river.

Early the next morning, Nykola rushed to his favourite fishing spot, just to see what he would see. Suddenly out of the deep water the fish he had caught the previous day appeared near the shallow edge of the stream. It deposited a small yellow pebble on the shore. Nykola picked up the pebble and was shocked to discover that it was a gold nugget.

"This is unbelievable," he thought. "Not only can the fish talk, but it also kept its promise of a reward for releasing it." Nykola caught no fish that day. He hid the gold nugget in a safe place, and wondered what the next day would bring.

Early the following morning he sat on his rock and prepared to cast his line into the water. Before he could do so, the fish swam up and deposited another gold nugget. Once again, he caught no fish that day.

On each of the next three days the same incredible thing happened. Each day that the fish brought another gold nugget, Nykola could not catch a fish. It almost seemed as though the fish was trading gold for the lives of the fish in his school.

On Sunday Nykola went to church, as usual; he never fished on Sundays. He had a total of five nuggets, which represented a small fortune. Nykola was now wealthy beyond his wildest dreams. This sudden wealth posed a problem, however.

How could he explain his good fortune to the people of the village? Telling the truth was out of the question. Nobody would believe him.

If he said that he had discovered the gold in the riverbed while fishing, he would create a gold rush, which could easily cause the destruction of the riverbank, and the feverish hunt for the gold was sure to cause bad feelings among the villagers.

The lord of the village was also likely to take the gold from Nykola, and could even charge him with being a thief.

Nykola wrestled with this problem every waking moment. What to do? His good fortune caused him a lot of trouble. The well-intentioned act of the fish had turned into a very large problem. Nykola cursed the fish. Perhaps he should not have released it.

The solution to his dilemma was suddenly found when he awoke from a deep sleep, and realized that the whole episode was nothing more than a bizarre dream.

How the Dog
Found Himself a Master

The Dog was once his own master, and he lived the way the Wolf does, in freedom. One day the Dog thought to himself, "I am tired of wandering around all the time looking for food. I am tired of always worrying about those animals who are stronger than I am. I am tired of this kind of life. I will hire myself out as a servant to the strongest creature on earth. Then he will protect me and feed me and I will serve him."

The Dog set out to find the strongest creature on earth. He walked until he met a Wolf, who was as strong as he was fierce.

"Where are you going?" asked the Wolf.

"I am looking for someone to serve. Would you like to be my master, Wolf?"

"Why not?" said the Wolf, and the two went on together.

They walked on until, suddenly, the Wolf stopped and stuck his nose into the air. He sniffed twice and then darted off the road and into the bushes. The Dog was very surprised.

"What are you doing, Master?" he asked.

"Do you not smell the Bear coming? He will eat up both of us," said the Wolf as he slunk off deeper into the forest.

The Dog left the Wolf and asked the Bear,

"Bear, I would like to enter your service; will you be my master?"

"I should think so," said the Bear. "I would like a servant. Let us go find a herd of cattle so that we may celebrate our partnership with a good meal."

The two found a herd of cattle, but were startled to hear a great and terrible roaring. All the cattle were bawling loudly and running in a panic all over the field. The Bear peered around a tree and then took to his heels, running for all he was worth into the forest.

The Dog asked the cattle what the great noise and the panic were all about.

"It is the Lion!" they cried as they milled around in a crowd.

"Lion? Who is the Lion?" asked the Dog.

"Do you not know? The Lion is the King of the Beasts!"

"Then I will say good bye to the Bear," said the Dog. "I want for my master the strongest creature on earth."

The Dog went to the Lion and said, "Lion, will you be my master? I will serve you well."

The Lion agreed, and the Dog went with the Lion. With such a strong master the Dog was happy, and he served the Lion for a long time. It was a good life for the Dog. He had plenty to eat and nobody in the forest dared to touch him, for his master was the Lion.

One day the Lion and the Dog were walking along the path when, suddenly, the Lion stopped, sniffed, and struck the ground angrily with his paw. The Dog came to him and asked what was the matter.

"I smell a Man approaching," said the Lion. "We had better go and hide someplace until he is gone."

"Well, if you fear this Man, I will say good bye to you," said the Dog. "I want for my master the strongest one on earth."

The Dog went to the Man and asked to serve him. The Man agreed and the two went off together. Since then, to this very day, the Dog still serves the Man and knows no other master.

How the Saints Ate Cream

Once a priest had a servant named Ivan. Priests, as usual, fed their servants poorly. They gave them only stale bread, and the servants were always hungry.

One evening a rich man brought his daughter to be baptized. Ivan watched where the servant girl put the bread the rich man had brought, took a loaf and put it into his sack. Then he thought, "Am I stupid that I eat only bread? Wait! I shall try to get myself some cream from the cellar!"

The servant girl dozed off and Ivan, with the bread, descended into the cellar. He sat by the bowl of cream and ate his fill. In the darkness, however, he dripped some cream onto the floor.

In the morning the wife of the priest opened the cellar and saw that someone had eaten the cream. The wife suspected Ivan and began to complain to the priest, saying, "Ivan is stealing from us."

The priest called Ivan and said, "Ivan, why are you trying to cause trouble?"

Ivan said, "I never troubled anyone before, Father, so why would I start now?"

The priest said, "Well, what, maybe it was the saints who ate the cream?"

"Who knows?" said Ivan. "Maybe it was the saints."

The next day Ivan took the key to the church and the large bowl of cream and went to the church, where he rubbed the mouths of the statues of the saints with cream. He wiped them all once, but for St Nicholas the Magician, the eldest of all, he smeared even the beard. He locked up the church and went off.

In the morning the wife of the priest went into the cellar and saw that the large bowl of cream was missing.

She again complained to the priest, "Ivan is stealing cream again. He even took the bowl."

The priest asked Ivan, "Did you do this?"

"Not I, Father."

"No? Was it perhaps the saints again?"

Ivan said, "Why, yes, of course. It was the saints again."

The priest wanted to say more, but he had to go to the church, as he could hear the sexton ringing the bell for service. The priest, when he entered the church, saw all the saints with their faces smeared with cream.

The priest quickly locked the church and told the sexton, "Do not ring the bell. There is no service today."

He ran home and called to his wife, saying, "The situation is bad. The saints really did eat the cream."

The priest told his wife and Ivan that they all had to go to the church to see the saints. The wife said, "Wait, Ivan! Take the whip, just in case."

Ivan took the whip, and they went to the church. The priest opened the doors and they all went in. As soon as the wife saw the saints with the cream, she said, "Ivan, beat all the saints soundly, but beat Nicholas the Magician twice. He led them to it!"

Ivan beat all the saints but he beat Nicholas the Magician three times. They then went home.

That night, Ivan took the key to the church, quietly opened the door and hid all the saints in the loft. As the next day was a feast day, the priest awoke early and went to the church to prepare for the service. Not a single saint was in his place! The priest became afraid. "What is happening?" he cried. "The saints have fled the church!"

He ran home and yelled, "Ivan! Ivan! Did you not see?"

"See what?" said Ivan.

"The saints have all left the church!"

"Oh yes, I saw," said Ivan "They came to the yard and wanted to see you, but you were sleeping and it was not proper to awaken you, so they ate breakfast and went on."

The priest immediately ran down the road where a woman was going for water.

"Listen, did you not see them?"

The woman, thinking the priest was talking about the party of surveyors who had come to parcel out some land, said, "Yes, I saw them. They went across the river and beyond the mountain."

The priest ran back to his yard and yelled, "Ivan, saddle a horse and chase after the saints! Whatever they want, I will give to them, just so they return!"

Ivan rode beyond the mountain and saw the surveyors and some villagers gathered there to parcel out the land. Ivan sat and talked with them for a while, and then rode back.

"Well? What?" asked the priest.

"They are insulted, Father. They said that they will not return until the priest pays each one of them three gold pieces and Nicholas the Magician six gold pieces, and a quarter-barrel of whisky and a large bowl of varenyky with cream. They said that they will come only in the night so that no one will see them. That seems to be honorable."

The priest said, "Good! Chase after them and tell them that everything will be done as long as they return."

Ivan rode beyond the mountain, talked to the villagers for a while, returned and said, "They said they will return tonight. They said to prepare everything in the yard."

The priest prepared the money and the whisky and waited. His wife set out a large bowl of varenyky with cream.

They waited and waited. It was already midnight, but the saints were not there, nor were they coming.

The priest said, "Ivan, my wife and I are going to go to sleep for a bit. You wake us when they come." And the priest immediately began to snore.

Ivan ate the varenyky with cream, took the gold and hid the whisky. Then he took the saints down from the loft, washed them and placed them again in the church. Finally, he himself lay down to sleep.

The priest awoke, saw it was morning and jumped up. "Why has Ivan not awakened me?"

He saw that Ivan was sleeping and the varenyky had been eaten and he yelled, "Ivan! Ivan! Get up!"

Ivan finally woke up. The priest asked, "Have the saints come? Where are they?"

"Yes, they came. They ate, drank, treated me and went into the church."

"Why did you not wake me?"

"I was going to, but Nicholas the Magician said, 'Do not wake Father. He just fell asleep and will be very angry if you wake him.'"

69

The Lion and the Mosquitoes

One day a Lion was sitting under a bush lazily looking around him. He saw some Mosquitoes buzzing around nearby.

"I am happy that I am so big and strong that I need fear no one," he said. "Not like these wretched little Mosquitoes who are afraid of everyone, for there is no one in the world who cannot crush them."

The Mosquitoes heard the Lion, and they were angered by his contemptuous words.

"Do not think that no one can get the better of you, Lion," said one Mosquito. "Just because you are big and strong is no reason to think that you are better than we are. We might just prove to be more than you can handle, if we wish."

"Ho, ho!" laughed the Lion. "I could crush all of you with one little paw! It is you who had better be careful of what you say, or I will take care of you."

This angered the Mosquitoes even more.

"Come, friends," said another Mosquito. "Let us show this Lion how we can fix him. He will never laugh at us again."

The Mosquitoes flew at the Lion and began to bite him everywhere. Although the Lion swatted at the Mosquitoes, they were too quick for him and there were too many. They stung him mercilessly.

The Lion jumped up into the air and ran around in circles, but the Mosquitoes flew after him. He rolled on the ground, but they flew up and then landed on him when he stopped. He ran to the pond and sank himself under the water, but he still had to breathe. When he put his nose out of the water, the Mosquitoes stung him till his nose swelled up tight.

Finally the Lion feared for his life and he began to plead with his tormentors.

"Please leave me alone," he whined. "I did not mean to make fun of you, and I will never do it again."

The Mosquitoes rose in a cloud and said, "May this teach you a lesson, Lion. Never again boast of your strength or your wisdom."

❖

The Mayor of Durak

When Vuiko Boyko got old and had only a few teeth left in his head, he liked to tell this story to anyone who would listen:

"Long ago, when I was still a young fellow wandering around the world seeking my fortune, I came to a town called Durak. You would like it there; the more a man is a fool, the more he is liked. The biggest fool of all usually becomes mayor.

"When I first got to the town, I passed by the mayor himself, who was riding in his carriage away from the town. I went right to his mansion in the central square, where I spoke to his wife.

"I said, 'Madam, your husband has just left on a trip around the world. He will not return to this town, and he has sent me here to take care of his worldly possessions.'

"She was not at all surprised by what I had just told her. I said, 'The first thing we must do is cut down these two big chestnut trees. They block the sun from the house.'

"Although she must have been fond of those two massive trees in front of the house, she said nothing. Down they came.

"That evening the mayor came home. He stopped and stared at his house and said to himself, 'Now, this is a strange thing. This is where my house ought to be, but this is not my house; my house has two big chestnut trees in front. This house has no trees, so it cannot be my house. This town looks like Durak, but it cannot be, because my house is in Durak, and my house is not here. I must have come to the wrong town.'

"The mayor rode off and went looking for Durak, and I guess he is still looking, for nobody has seen him since. And that is how I became the mayor of Durak."

The Mice and the Rooster

Once there lived together two Mice and a Rooster. The Mice were carefree and spent their days playing and running about, while the Rooster was industrious. Any work that had to be done was done by him, and he woke everyone with his crowing every day at dawn.

One day the Rooster was sweeping the yard when he found a ripe stalk of wheat growing there.

"Come, Mice, come see what I have found!" he called.

The two Mice came running.

"Oh, look!" they cried. "It is a stalk of wheat. Now we can have some cookies. But first it must be harvested and threshed."

"Who will do it?" asked the Rooster.

"Not I," said one Mouse.

"Not I," said the other Mouse.

"Then I will do it myself," said the Rooster.

He set to work while the Mice ran off to their games. He harvested the wheat and threshed it.

"Come, Mice, come and look at the wheat I have threshed," he called.

The Mice came running.

"Oh, that is very fine wheat," they said. "Now it must be taken to the mill and ground into flour."

"Who will do it?" asked the Rooster.

"Not I," said one Mouse.

"Not I," said the other Mouse.

"Then I will do it myself," said the Rooster.

He threw the bag of grain over his shoulder and took it to the mill. The Mice carried on singing and dancing and playing. When he returned from the mill, the Rooster called to the Mice.

"Come, Mice, come and see the flour."

"Well done," said the Mice. "Now the flour must be made into dough and the cookies must be baked."

"Who will do it?" asked the Rooster.

"Not I," said one Mouse.

"Not I," said the other Mouse.

"Then I will do it myself," said the Rooster.

He made the dough, lit the pich and put the cookies in to bake while the Mice played outside in the yard. When the cookies were baked the Rooster put them on the windowsill to cool. The Mice immediately smelled them and came running.

"How good they smell!" said one Mouse.

"And I am so hungry!" said the other one.

"Wait!" cried the Rooster. "Who was it who found the wheat?"

"You did," said the Mice.

"And who harvested it and threshed it?"

"You did," said the Mice, more quietly.

"And who took the grain to the mill and had it ground?"

"You did," they said in a small voice.

"And who made the dough and lit the fire and did the baking?"

"You did," said the Mice in a tiny voice.

"And what were you two doing all this time?" asked the Rooster.

The two Mice said nothing. They hung their heads and crept sheepishly out the door.

"Lazy Mice such as you do not deserve cookies," said the Rooster, and he ate up all the cookies himself.

The Miracle of the Fire

In a certain village lived two brothers, one of whom was very rich and the other very poor. As is often the case with such people, the rich brother was a greedy sort, while the poor brother was a kind and gentle man.

Jesus and His disciples were in the area and, after a day of preaching to the people, they stopped to rest near some trees at the edge of the village. Being hungry, they started a fire to cook their food.

On this evening, the fire had died out in the stove of the poor brother. His wife saw the glow of the fire near the trees and sent her husband to get some embers to start a fire in their stove. The husband approached the group and said, "Greetings, friends. The fire in my stove has gone out, and I was wondering if I could have some embers to start it again."

Jesus did not introduce His group to the poor brother, but said, "Certainly. Take as many embers as you need."

"I thank you," said the brother, "but I appear to have forgotten to bring a container for the embers."

Jesus replied, "You can safely take the embers in your cap. It will not burn. Also, if you need some money, place some embers in the four corners of your house, leave the house for a short time, and when you return you will find coins in place of the embers."

The brother, being a trusting soul, did as he was told and, indeed, the embers did not burn his cap. Arriving home, he started the fire, and his wife prepared a meagre supper.

While they ate, he told his wife what he had been told to do with the embers if they wanted some money. His wife was not too sure about this strange idea, but finally went along with her husband.

He placed a few embers in each corner of the house, and they left, looking back often. They waited a while and, seeing no smoke, they went back to the house and were surprised to see the embers replaced with coins. They scooped up the coins and placed them in a heap on the table.

At this moment the next-door neighbours paid them a visit, as often happened. They explained to the neighbors what had happened, and soon the whole village knew about the event, including the rich brother.

The rich brother came visiting with a basket of food, pretending to be kind. But to the bottom of the basket he had pasted some sticky tar so that, as he placed the basket on the table over the coins, some of the coins stuck to the tar. In this way he was able to steal some of the coins. His poor brother told him about the strangers camped near the trees where the fire was burning.

Immediately the rich brother went up to the group of men and asked for some embers, making up a story about his fire having gone out. Of course, Jesus knew what he was up to, and told him to help himself to the embers.

The rich brother scooped his container full of embers, hurried home and spread heaps of embers in all the four corners of his house and all the other buildings. Immediately, the embers burst into flame and the house and buildings burned down to the ground.

The rich brother was now as poor as his brother had been. This was a punishment and a lesson: do not be greedy and selfish.

❖

86

The Phantom Turkey

Nykola was a young man who lived in a village in Southwestern Ukraine near the River Prut. He frequently visited his friend Anton who lived in a village some distance away. Walking there, he would pass the house his father lived in, going down the lane that went between the yard of his father and that of the neighbor, whose name was Karl. Stout woven willow fences ran along both sides of the lane.

Karl had a large bamboo plant growing in one corner of his garden. This plant, being very prolific, had spread quickly in all directions and filled the garden. It was not long before the bamboo crept under the fence and began to fill the lane between the fences. Nykola decided to cut the bamboo before it blocked the lane completely. He thought it would be best to discuss this with Karl.

"Oh, no. That is not a good idea," said Karl. "Anyone who cuts the bamboo down would release all sorts of evil spirits which live inside the hollow stems."

Nykola asked, "Why would you plant the bamboo in the first place if you knew it would be a problem to cut it later?"

"I did not plant the bamboo, and do not know how it appeared in my garden. Perhaps someone who does not like me planted it there, knowing that I believe in such spirits."

Try as he might, Nykola could not convince Karl that his fears were groundless. Karl warned Nykola that cutting the bamboo down would cause a lot of grief for him. In spite of the warning, Nykola decided to cut the bamboo in a few days.

One morning, Nykola took his axe and began to chop at the bamboo. Karl watched him, shaking his head. When the path was clear, Nykola gathered the cuttings and piled them up for burning.

That evening Nykola went to visit Anton and to tell him what had happened.

Anton was very dismayed when he heard what Nykola had to say. He also believed in the spirits Karl had spoken of. "I am very concerned for your safety, my friend," he said.

Nykola could not convince Anton that it was nothing more than superstition.

Late that evening, Nykola walked home in the light of a full moon. When he reached the spot where the bamboo once stood, Nykola had a weird feeling, the likes of which he had never felt before.

Just down the lane he saw an enormous turkey sitting on the fence. The huge bird made no sound, but kept staring at Nykola. Without hesitation, he swung his cane at the turkey with all his might. To his astonishment, the cane went right through the turkey as if through thin air. The turkey simply sat on the fence and stared at Nykola.

It did not take long for Nykola to reach the gate to his yard. As he reached for the latch, the gate opened by itself. The same thing happened when he tried to open the door to the house. It opened by itself and gently closed behind him, and there was no one else around. Even the turkey had not followed him.

Nykola broke into a cold sweat as he undressed and got into bed. Before he closed his eyes, he looked at the window, and there it was again. A large turkey head was staring at him through the window. He pulled the covers over his head and spent a sleepless night, thinking about the events of the past day.

Next day, Nykola raced to see Anton to tell him what had happened the night before. He did not tell his parents or his neighbour about the bamboo or the turkey. He trusted Anton to keep it a secret. Perhaps Anton could offer him some advice.

Anton listened to his friend with a feeling of grief and sympathized with him. After much discussion, it was decided to seek the help of a vorozhka who lived in a nearby village.

Everyone in the village knew where the vorozhka lived, although few people had ever been to see her. People who lived nearby avoided her, believing that she might be evil and wish to do them harm. However, they did not hesitate to seek her advice when strange events occurred in their lives.

While walking to her house, both young men discussed what they thought she was like, as neither had ever seen her. They agreed that she must be an ugly, toothless old hag dressed in tattered black clothes, and she must live in a rundown old hovel.

Reaching her village, the two friends asked a woman to direct them to her house. The woman hurriedly crossed herself as she pointed to the right house.

What the young men thought would be a dirty hovel turned out to be a small, neat cottage near the river. A strong willow fence protected a tidy garden of flowers and vegetables and a curved cobblestone path led to the door from the gate.

The appearance of the house certainly did not suggest that the owner was a hideous old crone. Feeling a little less fearful, Nykola knocked lightly on the cottage door and stepped back, not knowing what to expect.

The door opened, revealing a handsome young woman. Her black hair was neatly combed and tied in a large bun on the back of her head. Her eyes, which matched the color of her hair, and her olive complexion gave her a mysterious air. Overall, she was a beautiful young woman indeed!

She smiled at her callers and asked them in. Her manner and her charm put Nykola and Anton completely at ease.

"It is obvious," she said, "that you have a big problem. I am of Gypsy ancestry and have been blessed with certain powers that I cannot explain, but I am able to solve many problems that plague people now and then. And now, tell me the specific reason for your visit to my humble cottage."

She listened intently as Nykola told her the whole story.

"If you had come to me before you cut the bamboo down, and heeded the warning of your friends, I could have helped you do the job properly. However, the problem can be solved, but it will take some work to rid you of the phantom turkey."

"I will do anything you say, as long as I am rid of this terrible situation. And what will I pay you for your services?" asked Nykola.

"Because I earn my living from a God-given power bestowed upon me, I ask only that you be the judge of what you think the solution to your problem is worth," she replied.

"Fair enough," Nykola responded. "Now, please tell me what I must do."

"This will not be simple, but you must do exactly as I tell you. You must go to the cemetery, and remove enough soil from the grave of one of your ancestors to fill a jar I will give you. This must be done at midnight during a full moon.

"Bring the jar to me the day after it is filled, and I will tell you what you must do next. Your friend Anton may assist you, but you must tell no one else."

"This I promise to do," said Nykola. "And is there a way I could help my neighbour to get rid of the bamboo on his property?"

"Yes, there is, but we will deal with that situation after you rid yourself of your immediate problem."

Nykola and Anton left the cottage in high spirits, relieved that the difficulty Nykola faced would soon be over. Anton did not say, "I told you so," and Nykola did not offer any comments, at least not at this point.

Nykola stayed with Anton until the next full moon. He did not want to risk facing the ghostly turkey again. He prayed fervently that the procedure outlined by the vorozhka would be successful.

Anton and Nykola went to the cemetery when the next full moon had risen in the sky. It cast strange shadows across the monuments and burial mounds. With beating hearts they crept to the grave they had chosen and looked about, crossing themselves all the while.

Quickly, Nykola gathered enough soil from the grave to fill the jar, and then both young men crossed themselves again and ran home as fast as they could.

Early the next morning they rushed to the cottage to deliver the soil to the vorozhka. She took the jar to a room in the back of the cottage and closed the door. Nykola and Anton could hear her uttering an incantation that lasted for some time. When she finally appeared, she was carrying two jars in her hands. Speaking to Nykola, she explained:

"I have divided the soil into two parts, adding special items to both. The one in my right hand must be used to rid yourself of the phantom turkey. When you leave your friend tonight, you must go home in the dark as you did when the turkey first appeared. The turkey will certainly appear. When it does, throw the soil from the jar at the turkey, and the turkey will vanish. Spread what is left of the soil on the ground where you cut the bamboo down. Your problem will be solved.

"The second jar will be used to ward off the spirits when your neighbour cuts down the bamboo on his property. Get your father and the neighbour together and tell them exactly what happened to you when you cut the bamboo down. They will believe everything you tell them, I assure you. Your neighbour must scatter the contents of the second jar over the bamboo in his garden, making sure that some soil touches every stem. Tell him to cut the bamboo down and burn it in the same spot where it originally grew."

That night, as Nykola walked home, the phantom turkey appeared on the fence ahead. It sat and stared at Nykola, who threw the soil at it. As he did so, the turkey vanished. He then spread the remainder of the soil on the ground where he had cut down the bamboo.

Next day, Nykola and his father helped Karl rid the garden of the bamboo, and nothing unusual happened. Although Nykola did not believe in the supernatural or any other form of mystical events, he admitted that there are some unexplainable things that do happen from time to time.

Nykola and Anton visited the vorozhka once more to pay her for the work she had done. Nykola apologized for the small payment, saying that it was all he could afford.

The vorozhka accepted his offering and assured him that under the circumstances she did not expect more.

Seven Rooks and Their Sister

There lived in this world a man and wife, and they had seven sons. These brothers did not live in peace. They always warred and fought amongst themselves, and their mother was angry at them because of it.

One day, when the father had gone to the forest for wood and the mother was left at home with the boys, they fought so much and she became so angry at them that she did not know how to curse them enough. Out of anger she cried, "May you turn into rooks!"

She had not finished saying this before the boys become rooks and disappeared far into the forest. Coming to an abandoned house, they alit and in this house again became human. They settled there and began to work together, living as friends, sharing the household chores.

Among them was one brother so clever that he was able to make muskets for all of them. They went hunting and shot all sorts of food. From this they had meat, while for bread they worked for wages. Whatever tools they needed, they made themselves.

The mother cried long and bitterly when the sons flew away from home. She had spoken without thinking and did not believe it would truly happen.

"If only I could have one child for comfort," she grieved.

A daughter was born to her, and thirteen years passed since the boys had flown away. As the girl grew older and drove the cattle to the pasture, the other children teased her and called her a rook because her brothers had become rooks.

The girl heard so much about her brothers that she decided to go out into the wide world in search of them. She went far into the forest, so far that it was impossible to return. Wandering there, she stumbled onto a house where the old mother of the Moon lived.

"From where are you, child? Stay and live here with me," the mother of the Moon said.

"It is not possible for me to live here, because I am searching for my brothers," answered the girl. "Do you perhaps know where they are?"

"No, I do not know where your brothers live," the mother of the Moon told the girl, "but soon my son will come home and I shall ask him in which land your brothers live."

The young Moon came home, was asked the question by his mother and replied, "I have not been there yet, but it seems that they live in the land where the Sun dances."

The next day, the mother of the Moon, having fed the girl, told the Moon to lead her to the Sun. The girl came to the house of the Sun, where lived the old mother of the Sun.

"Where are you going?" she asked the girl.

"I go into the world to search for my brothers, whom my mother cursed. They turned into rooks and flew away," the girl answered. "Do you know where they are?"

"I have not heard anything about this. Maybe the Sun knows," said the old mother of the Sun.

The Sun came home, and the mother asked him about the brothers.

"No, I do not know," the Sun replied. "Most probably, I have not warmed the land in that far country. Maybe the Wind knows."

The mother of the Sun fed the girl and asked the Sun to lead her to the mother of the Wind. Soon they came to the mother of the Wind. She also fed the girl and asked where she was going.

"I am searching for my seven lost brothers," the girl replied.

The mother of the Wind also had not heard about them, and when her son came home, she asked him if he knew in which land lived the seven brothers who became rooks.

"I know," said the Wind, "because when the rain drenched me, I took off my slippers and hung them to dry near the chimney of these brothers. I must return to get my slippers when they are dry."

The mother of the Wind said to her son, "There is a girl here who calls these seven rooks her brothers. You must take her to them."

In the morning the girl arose, the mother of the Wind fed her, and then the Wind took her on his back to the house where her brothers lived. They were not home at the time, having gone into the forest with their rifles. The Wind left the girl there, took his slippers and went on to dance over the world.

In the oven the girl saw a pot with food. She ate some and then crawled beneath the bed of the youngest brother and fell asleep.

At noon, the brothers returned home. The youngest of them, who was cooking the food that day, took the meal out of the oven and noticed that it had been touched.

"Aha, my brothers. It seems that someone has tasted our dinner," he said.

"Who could have tasted it?" the brothers asked. "We have lived alone for so many years, and beyond ourselves, we have not seen anyone else here."

They ate their lunch and then again left. The second brother stayed behind to cook supper. Having prepared the meal, he went into the forest to join his brothers. When he had left the house, the girl came out of hiding, ate a bit of the meal and again hid herself, but this time she crawled beneath the bed of the second brother. She again fell asleep.

When the brothers gathered for supper, the second brother noticed that the meal had been touched.

"Definitely, someone tasted it," he told the other brothers.

"You are wrong. It just seems that way to you," said the third brother.

They ate supper and lay down to sleep. One of them dreamed that their sister had come for a visit. When they awoke in the morning, he told them his dream.

After preparing their lunch and having their breakfast, the brothers went off to work. The girl came out of her hiding place, cleaned up the house, ate some of the lunch and then again hid, this time beneath the bed of the third brother. At noon the brothers gathered for their midday meal.

"Again brothers, there is less food. It seems someone samples it in small amounts," said the third brother, who had cooked lunch.

"But who is there to sample the food, when we have lived here for so many years and in that time have not seen a single living person in these lands?" said the other brothers.

After eating lunch, they again went into the forest. The fourth brother stayed behind to cook supper and, after cooking it, he followed the others.

That evening they gathered at home for supper, but saw that again there was less food than was cooked. They sat down and talked among themselves.

"What a wonder. A number of times now someone has had breakfast, lunch and supper with us. There is someone here with us. Let us look for him."

They began to look about the house, and then peeked beneath the beds. Under the bed of the fourth brother they found the girl.

"Get up, girl. What are you looking for here?" they asked of her.

"I search for my brothers, whom my mother cursed, asking that they be turned into rooks, and thus it happened. This my father told me, although he was not home at the time. He had gone to the forest for wood," she began to explain to the brothers.

"If your brothers have become rooks, why have you left your parents?" they asked the girl.

"Because the children taunted me, calling me a rook when I drove the cattle to pasture."

The brothers felt certain that the girl was telling the truth.

"You could stay here with us," they told her. "You can cook for us and keep house, and together we shall go hunting."

She stayed in the house with her brothers, and began to keep house for them. The brothers were very friendly towards her, honored her and dressed her in luxurious clothes, which suited a young, beautiful girl.

They constantly thought about how to return home. They feared that, once they left the house in the forest, they would again turn into rooks.

After three years had passed peacefully, a great misfortune occurred in the forest. One of the brothers killed a wild goat, but it was not a wild goat; it was really the daughter of the witch Baba Yaha. When she found out her daughter was dead, Baba Yaha swore that she would revenge herself on the brothers.

One day when the girl was at home alone, the evil witch appeared, bringing with her some coral beads. She showed them to the girl through the window and said, "Maybe you would buy these beads from me?"

"Good," answered the girl. She gave some money to the witch, who took it and went on her way. When the girl put the beads around her neck, they immediately choked her.

The brothers returned home for lunch and saw that their sister lay still on the floor. They gathered about her, found the beads around her neck and broke them apart, and she started to breathe slowly. Then they began to rub her body and save her from death. When she got up, the brothers told her not to show herself to anyone, ever.

Again she began to look after the house as before. They lived well. Half a year passed when the evil witch again appeared. She brought with her a fine red apple and said, "Maybe you desire an apple. Here it is for you."

The girl took some money and bought the apple. She bit a sliver and collapsed onto the floor. Barely was it visible that she lived, as she breathed but rarely.

The brothers returned from the field and tried to find what had harmed their sister a second time. They looked but found nothing. They were very sorry for their sister but what could they do?

They made a coffin from crystal with silver chains. They placed their dead sister in the coffin, but did not bury it in the ground. They hung it in the forest, like a cradle, between two trees. They themselves, out of sorrow for their sister, went into the wide world following their eyes. They wanted to find their parents and tell them that they could not protect their sister.

Shortly after, the young son of the tsar, with his servant, went hunting in the forest and became lost. They wandered through the forest for three months and, in that time, they did not see one living soul.

Then, one night, they camped near the place where the crystal coffin hung between the trees. During the night, the tsarevich saw something shining through the trees, and he said to his servant, "Let us go see what is flickering among the trees."

They went to the spot and found the crystal coffin. In it they saw a beautiful girl. Looking at her, they thought she might be only sleeping, as she did not appear to be dead.

The tsarevich ordered his servant to untie the chains from the trees and lower the coffin to the ground. When he untied a chain, it slipped out of his hands and the coffin fell so hard that the little sliver of apple was jarred from the mouth of the girl.

She awoke and told the tsarevich what had happened; then she led them to the house where she had lived with her brothers. But the brothers were not there and the house was abandoned. The tsarevich then decided to take the girl with him.

Soon after, he married the girl, but he had a stepmother who hated him.

She told the tsar, her husband, "Do you see what your son is doing? He found himself a beggar girl of some sort and married her. How can we keep a beggar in our rooms?"

The stepmother wanted to rid the world of her stepson and daughter-in-law, but she was not at all successful, because the tsarevich loved his wife and looked after her as if she were his own eye.

"If your son will not kill his wife, then you must kill them both," said the stepmother to the tsar. "If you do not do this, then I am not a wife to you, and you are not a husband to me."

The tsar feared his wife and usually did all that she wanted.

With a heavy heart, the tsar spoke to his son, "Listen to me, my son. If you do not return your wife to where you found her and kill her, and then bring me her heart and eyes, then I shall have to kill you both myself."

The tsarevich cried bitterly and went with his wife to the edge of the world. After them ran the favorite hound of the tsar. The tsarevich killed the hound and took its heart and eyes, intending to tell his father that they were those of the girl.

His young wife said to him, "If this is to be my fate, then step away from me. I shall go myself into the wide world, following my eyes."

And she departed, crying. "Now," she thought, "I shall go to the house where I lived with my brothers and live there, for a child will soon be born to me."

Time passed and she gave birth to twins, both boys. And her sons were beautiful. One had on his forehead the sign of the Sun, while the other had the sign of the Moon.

Time passed and the old tsar and the stepmother died. The son was now ruler, but it was not pleasant to rule without his spouse. "If I only knew where she is now," he said to himself, and he began to punish himself for what he did to her.

"Let us look for her," the young tsar said.

He and his servant searched the forest. At twilight they reached the place where they had found her in the crystal coffin. Remembering that nearby was the house where the brothers had lived, they went there together.

In the house they found a woman with two boys. The woman was wrapped in a kerchief so that her face was not visible. She welcomed them, laid out a bed for the tsar, and prepared a spot for the servant on the floor. She lay down herself on the bench and placed both children on the warm pich.

The whole night a candle burned on the table in the house.

It was pleasant for the young tsar to sleep on the bed, but it was not so good for the servant on the hard floor and he often awoke in the night. When the tsar fell asleep, one of his hands fell to the floor. One of the boys began to cry and call for his mother and she answered as if to herself, "Do not cry, son, I shall be with you soon. You must place the hand of your father back onto the bed."

The servant heard this.

In the morning, the woman arose quickly to cook breakfast for her guests. The tsar and his servant awoke, had breakfast and then went into the forest. They returned to the place where the coffin had been.

Here the tsar told the servant, "Oh, it is difficult to live on this earth. You know, if I saw my wife, it seems my heart would immediately become lighter and happier."

"But would you recognize her if you saw her?" he asked the tsar.

"I would recognize her," was the reply. "Even the lady where we spent the night is somewhat similar to her."

"While you slept, your hand hung down and she told her child, 'Do not cry, son, I shall be with you soon. You must place the hand of your father back onto the bed.'"

"Truly?" the elated tsar cried. "Let us wait here and near nightfall let us spend the night there again."

Nightfall came and they returned to the house in the forest. The woman shook with happiness as she made the same preparations as the night before.

Soon the tsar purposely hung his hand down. The woman arose, took his hand and put it by his side as was proper. Then he arose and embraced her, pleading for her to forgive him.

They returned home with their children. They had a large banquet, where all the people danced and were happy. At that exact time, into the city came seven brothers who were rooks.

"What kind of wedding is this?" they asked the people.

"The tsar has found his lost wife," they were told. "Look how young and good and beautiful she is!"

The brothers looked and realized that it was their sister. They had a joyful reunion, and everyone was happy again.

"Bring our aged parents here so that they may rest near us," the tsarina said.

The brothers went to fetch their parents, and they all lived in peace and well-being.

❖

The Swan, the Pike
and the Crayfish

One day a Swan was swimming along on the river when a Pike called out to him, "Swan, where do you go when the river freezes?"

"Why do you want to know that, Pike?"

"I would like to go someplace warmer for the winter. There is not much air to breathe when the ice freezes the river over."

"I go to a warmer climate as soon as it gets too cold here," said the Swan. "I stay there until spring arrives here."

"Please take me with you," said the Pike.

"Very well," said the Swan. "It will be more fun to travel together."

As they continued talking over their plans, a Crayfish popped out of the water and listened to them.

"Oh, please, take me with you," begged the Crayfish.

"I do not mind," said the Swan. "The more the merrier. We will not leave until autumn, so I will return at the end of the summer and we can get ourselves ready to go."

The Swan flew off, never dreaming that the Pike and the Crayfish could not fly as well as he could.

When autumn arrived, the Swan returned to the river, found the Pike and told him, "Autumn has arrived and it is time for us to fly to the warm climate. Be ready to leave early tomorrow morning."

The Pike swam off to find the Crayfish and tell him the news.

"What will we do for food along the way?" asked the Crayfish.

"I suppose we will have to take enough along with us to last till the end of the trip," said the Pike.

"And how will we carry the food?" asked the Crayfish.

"We can carry it in a cart," said the Pike. "We will harness ourselves to it and ask the Swan to help us pull it."

The two friends filled their cart with food and then made three rope harnesses to pull it. They then waited anxiously for the Swan, who arrived early the next morning.

"Are you two ready to go?" asked the Swan. "I am leaving at once."

"We are ready," said the Pike. "But please help us to pull the cart with our food in it. We have three harnesses ready."

The Swan was surprised by this, but he was always ready to help.

"Very well," he said. "Tie the rope to my leg and I will pull."

The Crayfish looped one rope around the leg of the Swan and grabbed another with his claw. The Pike took the third rope in his mouth and the Crayfish cried, "All together now, pull!"

The three friends started to pull, each after his own fashion. The Crayfish scuttled jerkily backwards and helped himself along with his tail, the Pike jumped headfirst into the water, and the Swan strained his wings trying to rise into the air.

What a mess! The ropes broke from their struggles and the cart never budged. The three friends, meanwhile, shot forward when the ropes parted and they tumbled in all directions.

The only ones who thought that this was anything but a disaster were the frogs who were watching. They laughed and laughed and rolled around helplessly. They thought it hilarious that the Swan, the Pike and the Crayfish did not know better than to hitch themselves all to the same cart.

The Wolf and the Kids

Once a Goat and her Kids lived in a hut in the forest. Each morning Mother Goat would go to the meadow to graze on the fresh green grass, and she would leave her Kids at home with instructions not to open the door for anyone but her. When she returned to the hut, Mother Goat would sing:

> "My Kiddies small, my Kiddies dear,
> Open the door, for your Mother is here.
> Let me in and I will give you a treat,
> For I bring you milk both rich and sweet."

The Kids would know that this was their Mother, and they would rush to let her in. Mother Goat would feed them some milk and then leave again to graze until evening, when she would return to spend the night in the hut.

121

There was a hungry Wolf who lived nearby. One day he happened to see Mother Goat singing to her Kids. When he saw the door open, he decided that he would try to get into the hut the same way. Later, when Mother Goat was away, he went to the hut and sang:

"Open the door, my Kiddies, do,
For Mother is here with milk for you.
Let me in to get a treat,
For my milk is rich and sweet."

The Kids replied, "Whoever you are, we will not let you in. Your voice is rough and gruff, while our Mother sings in a soft and sweet voice."

The Wolf slunk off into the bushes to think about things. He thought that he would try again, but in a much softer voice. He went back to the hut and sang in the sweetest voice he could manage:

"Open the door, my Kiddies, do,
For Mother is here with milk for you.
Let me in to get a treat,
For my milk is rich and sweet."

The Kids replied, "Whoever you are, we will not let you in. Your voice is not thin and sweet like the voice of our Mother, and the words of your song are not right. Go away and leave us alone."

The Wolf again slunk off into the bushes. He hid himself and waited for Mother Goat to return, so that he could hear her better and learn how to imitate her. Soon Mother Goat came home and sang:

"My Kiddies small, my Kiddies dear,
Open the door, for your Mother is here.
Let me in and I will give you a treat,
For I bring you milk both rich and sweet."

The Kids knew right away that this was their Mother and they opened the door to let her in. As soon as she came in they told her that someone had been coming to the door trying to trick them. Mother Goat fed the Kids and praised them for not letting the stranger in.

Next morning Mother Goat again warned the Kids not to let anyone in but her. To make sure they knew her song exactly, she sang it to them twice more and then went off to graze in the meadow.

The Wolf spent the whole night practicing his song, but he could not get his voice to sound like a Goat. His voice was simply too rough and gruff. As he was practicing, a Fox came by and asked, "Why are you howling, Wolf? Are you in some pain?"

"I am singing, Little Sister Fox," said the Wolf. "I have found a hut full of Kids, and I am trying to get them to open the door by singing like their Mother. They know her voice, and I cannot get mine to sound like hers."

"You are not doing it right," said the Fox. "If you want to get at the Kids, I can show you what to do."

"Oh, could you, Little Sister Fox?" said the Wolf. "I would be so grateful if you would help me."

"What will I get from you if I help you, Brother Wolf?"

"When I catch those Kids, I will give you one of them," said the Wolf.

"Oh, no," replied the Fox. "You might take your time catching the Kids, and I am hungry right now. Go and find me a goose to eat and I will tell you what to do about your voice."

The Wolf agreed and ran off to find a goose. He spent a long time hunting along the edge of the river and finally managed to grab one. He ran back to the Fox, gave her the goose and said, "Now, Little Sister Fox, tell me what to do about my voice."

"Here is what you must do, Brother Wolf: you must go to the Blacksmith and tell him to forge you a new throat with a sweet voice. Then you will be able to sing like the bleating of Mother Goat."

"And where will I find this Blacksmith?" asked the Wolf.

"There is one on the edge of the village," replied the Fox.

The Wolf thanked the Fox and ran off to the village. He barged into the Blacksmith shop and said to the Smith, "I want you to make me a new throat so that I can sing like the bleating of a Goat."

"It can be done," replied the Blacksmith. "But how will you pay me?"

The Wolf said, "As you know, we animals have no money. Perhaps I could trade you something of value."

"Very well," said the Smith. "Bring me two live geese and I will do it."

The Wolf again ran off to the river and spent a long, long time hunting in and out of the bulrushes. He wound up soaking wet and miserable, but he was finally able to grab one goose, which he stuffed into a sack. He then returned to his hunting and, after a longer time, he caught a second goose.

The Wolf was very hungry indeed by this time, and he would have liked to eat the geese right then and there, but he needed them to pay the Blacksmith, so he chewed some bulrushes and went back to the Smith.

"I have brought your geese," said the Wolf. "Now be quick and forge me a new throat."

"Very well," said the Blacksmith. "Come up to the anvil, stick out your tongue as far as you can, and close your eyes. I will do the rest."

The Wolf came close to the anvil, stretched out his tongue as far as he could, closed his eyes, and stood there rigidly. The Blacksmith took a large hammer and struck the Wolf on the top of his head, killing him instantly. He then skinned the Wolf and sold the hide. He kept the geese in his yard and ate their eggs.

As for the Goat and her Kids, they remained alive and well, and were never bothered by any more Wolves.

Notes on the Tales

Page 11   Carrots to Coins

This story is not a common one. It was given to me by Michael Shklanka of Cochrane, Alberta, who heard it from his mother Anna. There are many stories of Jesus and the disciples in their travels; this one is fairly typical of them.

All too often people do not think to write down or record their stories, and then they are lost to all of us. To me, this is a genuine tragedy. The stories are a large part of who we are, and they teach those who follow about the culture and the traditions of the people who told the stories.

Sometimes people will tell me that their stories are too ordinary, and everyone knows them. Often, though, the person who knows the story could be the only person left alive who remembers the story. That is why it is so important to record every story or every part of a story that can be recalled. Let's not lose them!

Page 15   A Clever Trick

Here we have a classic example of a peasant outwitting not only the lord, but also the priest. These two represent authority, against whom the poor peasants were forever struggling.

Page 21   The Daughter of the Blacksmith

This is another of Anna Shklanka's stories that her son Michael passed along. The stories about Jesus often have as a moral that we should be thankful for what we have and not be greedy for that which is not meant for us.

Page 25   Death as a Godmother

This story came from the ancient battered book my father got from his father. He translated the story as best he could, but the first five pages were missing. Years later, I found a reprint of the same book in the library at Oseredok in Winnipeg, and J Zurowsky completed the translation. There exist several similar stories, but most of them have a male figure representing Death. In a very few stories, Death is female, as in this story.

Page 31   The Death of Kniaz Oleh

Nicholas J Sabulka of Salmon Arm, BC gave me a version of this story that his Dido used to tell, and Norman Harris translated a more classical version. This retelling is adapted from the two.

I suspect that non-Ukrainians will have trouble pronouncing "Kniaz," since the "k" is sounded, but there is really no equivalent in English. Although the word is often translated as

"Prince," it means much more than that. It means that Oleh was the supreme ruler of the country, and not just the son of a king.

Oleh ruled Kyivan Rus, which was the first state to arise among the Eastern Slavs. It was in the area around present-day Kyiv in Ukraine.

Page 35   The Fly that Plowed a Field

This story is similar to many of Aesop's fables. It is short and to the point, and it teaches a lesson to the listeners.

Page 39   The Fox and the Bear

There are many stories similar to this one, in many different areas of the world. Sometimes it is an old woman who fools a devil, but more often a fox outsmarts someone.

The appearance of corn indicates that there is likely at least one version from native America, since that is where corn originated.

Page 43   The Foxes in the Vineyard

This is another story like those of Aesop. Mother Fox knows the person she is dealing with, and can predict what he will do. For anyone who must live by their wits, this is a handy thing to be able to do.

Similar to other stories, this one is shorter than most of its sort. That sometimes happens with folk tales; a long story will become several short ones, or perhaps several compatible tales will be combined to make one very long one.

Nic Sabulka's Dido told this story many times, and it was always enjoyed no matter how many times it was told. It has a kind of a trick ending to solve a seemingly unsolvable puzzle. Most of the events in the story can be found in similar tales, but this is the only time I have run across this particular version.

Here is a story that explains how something came to be. There are many "explaining" stories, and most of them have a moral as well.

Once again we have a poor peasant getting the better of an authority figure. Of course, the authority figure is often portrayed as too stupid to be true, but that does not hinder the enjoyment the people derived from such a tale.

The life of a Ukrainian peasant was very hard, indeed, and as Lame Deer, the famous Sioux medicine man said, "A people who have so much to cry about as Indians do also need their laughter to survive." So it was with the Ukrainian peasant.

Page 71   The Lion and the Mosquitoes

Aesop's fables were certainly timeless, and they travelled to many lands, adapting to local conditions where possible. It is possible that this story changed when it came to Canada, since, although there aren't many lions here, there certainly are plenty of mosquitoes.

Page 75   The Mayor of Durak

The Wise Men of Gotham in England were fools such as those who lived in Durak. Where this story originated, we don't know, but it could have come from any place where people enjoy stories about fools.

Isaac Bashevis Singer wrote about *The Fools of Chelm and Their History.* Chelm is another town inhabited by fools, but it is placed in Russia.

Page 79   The Mice and the Rooster

This story is similar to the famous story of the grasshopper and the ants, and is familiar to children of many lands. Some such stories were simply translated into Ukrainian, and others were told so often that they became a part of the folklore of the country.

Page 83   The Miracle of the Fire

This is another story remembered by Michael Shklanka. His mother used to tell all kinds of stories, and we can only hope that Michael will come up with more of them.

The stories Michael submitted are stories I have never seen anywhere else. This points up the importance of collecting these stories while the people who remember them are still able to tell them. Too often people forget or die, and we lose their stories.

There is an apt African saying: "When an old man dies, an entire library goes with him."

Page 87   The Phantom Turkey

This is another of the stories Nic Sabulka's Dido told. The story is full of magic, but it all happens to ordinary people, not the princes and princesses we often find in folk tales. The appearance of real people lends truth to the story. Perhaps it really did happen! There are things in this world that cannot be explained.

Page 99   Seven Rooks and Their Sister

This is not a very common story. I have found it in only two Ukrainian-language collections, both of them translated by J Zurowsky.

The girl's search for her brothers takes her to all kinds of fantastic places and she meets many wonderful characters, all of which she takes in stride.

That is the way of folk tales — strange and magic things are accepted for what they are, and the story goes on with no trouble at all. Many things in some stories remain unexplained, but since they are not central to the story, they are allowed to happen.

This is also the first Ukrainian folk tale I have found that has as a character the famous Baba Yaha (or "Yaga"). She is a much more complex character than this story reveals, and I am sure we will see more of her as time goes on.

Page 117   The Swan, the Pike and the Crayfish

This is another Aesop-sounding tale, although it is longer than many of his works. It appears in several collections in both the Ukrainian and English languages.

Different translations of the same story often come out looking very dissimilar, all of which depends on who is doing the translating and who is doing the retelling. In my work, I usually adapt my retelling from the various versions that come my way. In some cases, I have seventeen or more versions of the same story.

Page 121   The Wolf and the Kids

There are many stories of wolves or foxes or dragons trying to speak like the mother or father of their intended victims, but they usually fail to work, and we learn not to try to be what we are not.

The repeated song is something the younger audience especially likes, as it is something that they can memorize and sing themselves.

—Danny Evanishen, Publisher

In this glossary:

[a] is pronounced as in far
[e] is pronounced as in get
[ee] is pronounced as in feet
[i] is pronounced as in sit
[o] is pronounced as between got and goat
[oo] is pronounced as in loose
[y] is pronounced as in yes

[kh] is pronounced as in Scottish loch
[zh] is pronounced as in vision